Sunworld

Leo P. Kelley

A Pacemaker® Book

Fearon Education
a division of
Pitman Learning, Inc.
Belmont, California

The SPACE POLICE™ Series

Prison Satellite	Backward in Time
Worlds Apart	Sunworld
Earth Two	Death Sentence

Editorial Director: Robert G. Bander
Managing Designer: Kauthar Hawkins
Cover and interior illustrator: Steven Hofheimer

Copyright © 1979 by Pitman Learning, Inc., 19 Davis Drive, Belmont, California 94002. Member of the Pitman Group. All rights reserved. No part of this book may be reproduced by any means, transmitted, or translated into a machine language without written permission from the publisher.

ISBN–0–8224–6381–4

Library of Congress Catalog Card Number: 79-51080

Printed in the United States of America.

1.9 8 7 6 5 4 3 2

CONTENTS

1. SPACE POLICE SCHOOL 1
2. PLAYING TRICKS 6
3. GRADUATION DAY 11
4. NOISY ALIENS 20
5. BATTLE AT SUNWORLD 28
6. A WATER CITY 35
7. VOICES FROM THE FUTURE 42
8. THE SUN GOES WILD 50

SPACE POLICE SCHOOL

The teacher stood in front of her class. She pointed to a star map.

She asked, "Who can tell me the name of this star?"

A man in the class said, "That looks like the star Varna to me."

The teacher asked, "What do the rest of you think? *Is* this the star Varna?"

A woman in the back of the room held up her hand. Her brown hair was cut short. The light in the room made it shine. Her eyes were as bright and blue as the sky on Earth.

The teacher said, "Yes, Ms. Brody? What do you think?"

"That's not the star Varna," Marsha Brody said. "The star Varna is light-years away from the part of space you're pointing to."

The teacher asked, "Then what is the name of this star?"

"That's not a star at all," Marsha Brody answered. "It's a space station."

"That's right," said the teacher. Then she pointed to the star map again. She asked more questions. The students in the class gave their answers. Most were right. A few were wrong. Every time Marsha gave an answer it was right.

After she had asked many questions, the teacher put the star map away. Then she turned back to her class. "This is your last day at the Space Police School," she said. "In fact, this is your last class. I've tried to teach you many things this year.

"Now I want to tell you one more thing. To be a good Space Police officer you've got to be smart. But that's not enough. You've also got to be careful. There are many worlds in space. Each of them is different. Strange things may

Space Police School 3

happen to you in those worlds. You must always remember to stay on your toes and think before you act."

While the teacher talked, some of the students listened. But others didn't listen. It wasn't that they thought their teacher was wrong. They knew she was right. But they had heard her say the same thing many times.

Marsha Brody listened to the teacher with only half her mind. With the other half she thought about the life she would start leading tomorrow. Tomorrow was graduation day at the Space Police School. Tomorrow Marsha would finally become a Space Police officer. She would no longer be Ms. Marsha Brody. She would be Officer Marsha Brody.

There had been times when Marsha was sure she wasn't going to make it. There had been times when her body had hurt because of the hard work she had to do. Other times she had thought she just couldn't learn even one more thing.

But her body had always stopped hurting. And she had learned more and more each day. Now her school days were almost over. Tomorrow they would be behind her.

". . . so you've got to be sharp and quick," the teacher was saying. "If you aren't, you might get into trouble. Never stop learning when you leave here. Once you've stopped learning, you've stopped being a good police officer."

The hands of the clock on the wall moved slowly. The words of the teacher went on and on. Finally a bell rang.

The teacher looked at the class. "That's all," she said. "I'll see all of you tomorrow at the graduation."

Marsha and the other students jumped to their feet. They picked up their books and papers. They all headed for the door. Then they rushed out of the room. In the hall some of the students spoke to Marsha. A man wished her luck in the new job she would get tomorrow. A woman called her Officer Brody which made Marsha smile.

Outside the sun was bright. Marsha looked around at the world she had lived on for the past two years. It was a world far away from Earth. Marsha had left Earth two years ago to come to the Space Police School. Tomorrow she would leave the school for a new world. She might be sent to any one of more than a hundred worlds in space. After graduation she would know which world she would work in.

Behind her, someone let out a happy yell. Marsha turned around. The man who had yelled was throwing his books up into the air. Then a woman near him did the same thing. Everyone laughed. Everyone was happy that school was over.

Soon Marsha left the other students. She made her way to the building she had lived in for the past two years. There was something she had to do.

When she got to her room, she began to look around. She looked under her bed. She looked behind her desk. She took a picture of her parents down from the wall and looked behind it. She looked under the sink.

Nothing anywhere, she thought. Maybe no one is going to play a trick on me tonight. On the last day of school, students always played tricks on one another. But Marsha didn't want to be taken by surprise. If some students planned to play a trick on her, she wanted to beat them at their own game. She wanted to find out about the trick before it was played on her.

PLAYING TRICKS

Once she was sure her room was OK, Marsha left it. She locked the door and went to get something to eat. After she had eaten, she returned to her room. The door was still locked. She opened it and went inside.

Everything in the room looked the same as it had before. She checked under the bed and sink again. Again she found nothing. She had been sure that someone would try to play a trick on her. She was happy no one had.

Marsha picked up a book and sat down to read. In a while she washed and got ready for bed. When she climbed in she pulled the sheet up—and let out a loud yell! Something hot had touched her feet!

She jumped out of bed. She pulled the sheet from the bed. Then she saw that someone had played a trick on her after all. Someone had put many tiny orange eggs in her bed—the eggs of the Bik-Bik bird. Marsha had seen eggs like these many times.

She reached for them. As she did, one hatched. The breaking shell gave off a flash of bright yellow light. Then another egg hatched. This time there was a flash of bright red light.

Marsha was too late. Before she could get the eggs out of her room they had all hatched. Flashes of colored light filled the room. Soon Bik-Bik birds of every color were running all around. They were fat little things with big eyes and small wings.

Suddenly, they all began to sing. Their song sounded like a machine that was breaking down.

Marsha put her hands over her ears to block out the noise they made. Then she ran to the window. She opened it. But none of the Bik-Bik birds flew out through the window. They just kept running around the room—singing.

Marsha couldn't stand the noise of their song. She picked up some of the Bik-Bik birds and threw them out the window. They flew away singing at the tops of their voices. Marsha threw more of the birds out the window. Then more. It took her a long time to get them all out of her room.

Then she sat down. She couldn't help laughing to herself. She thought she had been so careful. She had checked her room. But someone had gotten into her room. Someone had put the eggs of the Bik-Bik bird between her sheets.

Who? Who had gotten into her room? And *how* had that person gotten in?

Marsha remembered that the door of her room had been locked when she came back from her last class. And she had locked the door again when she went to get something to eat. It was still locked when she came back from dinner. Then she thought of something. Sure, her door had been locked all the time. But what about the window?

She smiled to herself. She had forgotten to lock her window. Someone must have come

Playing Tricks 9

into her room through the window. That someone had put the bird eggs between her sheets.

She went to her desk. She took her fingerprint set from it. She used the set to check the window for fingerprints. Then she took the fingerprints she had found to a room near her own. In the room was the space school's big computer.

Marsha put the card with the fingerprints on it into the computer. In less than a minute the computer told her who the fingerprints belonged to. Some were her own. But some were made by a friend of hers—Will Benson. Like Marsha, Will was a student at the Space Police School.

Marsha smiled to herself again. OK, Officer Benson, she thought. Now it's your turn. But what trick can I play?

She thought about it for a little while. Then she hit on an idea. Quickly she began to work on the computer. She made some changes in the wires that ran from the computer to the speaker in Will Benson's room. Then she went to his room. She stood outside his door and listened.

Inside the room the computer was teaching a lesson through the wall speaker.

"There are 110 worlds in our part of space," said the computer voice. "Tell me their names, please."

Marsha heard Will yell at the computer, "Be quiet!"

"That is not the right answer," said the computer voice. "Please try again."

Will yelled even louder, "Stop it! I'm trying to get some sleep!"

Marsha heard him trying to turn off his speaker. Then she heard him yell, "I can't turn off my speaker. It must be broken! Someone help me fix it!"

Marsha returned to her room. She was pretty sure Will wouldn't be able to turn off his speaker. She had changed the wires too much. She was sure that Will wouldn't get much sleep that night.

GRADUATION DAY

The next morning, Marsha went to the room where the graduation was to take place. She took a seat. She spoke to several of her friends. She asked them if anyone had seen Will Benson. No one had. She looked around the room. Will Benson wasn't in it. Just before graduation began, Marsha saw him come into the room. His eyes were red. He looked very tired. Marsha waved to him. He came over and sat down beside her.

Marsha asked him, "Didn't you sleep well last night? Your eyes are all red."

Will shook his head. "There was something wrong with the speaker in my room. The computer kept teaching a lesson all night long. I couldn't shut it off."

"Maybe some Bik-Bik birds got inside the computer," Marsha said. "Maybe they broke it."

Will looked at her in surprise. "You know?"

"Yes," Marsha said. "I know it was you who put the Bik-Bik bird eggs in my bed. I found your fingerprints on my window."

Will asked, "You're not mad at me, are you?"

"Not at all," Marsha answered. "You played a trick on me. So I played one on you."

"You mean—"

"I fixed the computer so it would teach a lesson through your speaker," Marsha told him. "And I fixed it so you wouldn't be able to turn it off."

"I should have guessed that," Will said, rubbing his face. "You know, I can hardly keep my eyes open."

Marsha laughed. So did Will. Then the graduation began.

The commander of the Space Police School spoke to the students. He told them that they

Graduation Day 13

had all done very good work during the past two years. He said that he hoped all of them would keep on doing good work now that they were becoming officers.

"I will if I don't go to sleep on the job," Will whispered.

Then the commander began to read the names of the students who had finished at the top of their class. Marsha's name was the second one that he read.

Will said, "Good for you, Officer Brody!"

A few minutes later the commander began to read the names of all the students. After he read each name he said where that new officer would work.

Will Benson found out that he would be working on the world named Stardown.

Marsha told him in a whisper, "That's wonderful! There are a lot of things going on on Stardown. You'll have an interesting job there."

"You said it! I can't wait to get there."

A few minutes later, Marsha heard her name read.

"Officer Marsha Brody," said the commander. "You will be working on Space Station

Number Nine for Commander John Kyle."

Marsha said in a low voice, "Oh, no! Not there."

Number Nine was one of ten stations in space. The police officers who worked there flew their ships through space looking for trouble and answering calls for help. Most space stations were well run and interesting places to be. But Number Nine was different.

"I'm sorry," Will said to her. "You should have been given a better job. I mean you had some of the highest marks in our class. What bad luck."

"You can say that again," she said. Her face was dark. She didn't look happy.

"Maybe it won't be so bad on Number Nine," Will said. "I've heard that some officers like Number Nine a lot."

"They can't be very good police officers if they do," Marsha said. She felt herself getting mad. Her face felt hot. "Number Nine hasn't been run right since Commander Kyle took it over."

"Well, there's one good thing about Number Nine," Will said.

Graduation Day 15

"There is? What is it?"

"You won't have to spend your whole life there," Will answered. "You can work there for a little while. Then you can ask to be sent to another place."

Marsha was about to say something. But just then the commander ended the graduation. The new officers all stood up. Then they left the room.

Outside the school, Marsha and Will shook hands. "Good luck to you," Marsha said.

"I just thought of another good thing about your new job," Will said to her.

"What is it?"

"There aren't any Bik-Bik birds on Space Station Number Nine."

Marsha smiled a little. But she really didn't feel like smiling. She felt more like yelling.

Soon Marsha and Will parted. Marsha went back to her room and packed her things. When she finished she got her laser gun. Then she went to the space field near the school.

The space field was crowded with students. All of them were taking ships to their new jobs on other worlds. Marsha waited with the others for the ship that would take her to Space Station Number Nine. Finally it came. When it started for the station, Marsha was on it.

The ship flew out into space. It flew for a long time. Its first stop was Space Station Number Nine. As the ship docked there, Marsha got up. Then she left the ship. She went through the air lock into the space station.

It was a very big place. Many police officers were at work. Marsha walked through the station looking for the office of Commander Kyle. It didn't take her long to find it.

The door of his office was open. Marsha put her things down outside the door and went in. A man sat behind a desk that had papers all over it. Some papers had fallen to the floor. They lay beside the desk. Marsha picked up the papers. She put them back on the desk.

"Thanks," said the man. He didn't look up.

"I'm Officer Marsha Brody from the Space Police School," Marsha said to him.

Then the man looked up. He had thick black hair and blue eyes. His face was space tanned. Marsha saw that his uniform was open at the neck.

"So you're the new gun," he said. He put his hands behind his head and sat back in his chair. He kept his eyes on Marsha.

She said, "The new gun? I'm afraid I don't understand."

"My new police officer," the man said. "You know—the new gun on this space station. By the way, I'm Commander Kyle."

"Yes, I know," Marsha said. She didn't smile.

"I can see you've heard something about me. Do they still say I don't know how to run a space station? Do they still put me down at the Space Police School?"

Marsha didn't say anything. She didn't know how to answer him.

Commander Kyle went on. "Some of the younger police officers don't like the way I run things. But I do OK. Let me welcome you to Space Station Number Nine."

"Thank you," Marsha said. She wished she could say that she was glad to be there. But that would be a lie.

She looked at Commander Kyle's uniform. He saw what she was looking at. He touched his neck where his uniform was open. "It gets pretty hot around here sometimes," he said.

Marsha thought about the world she had just left. It got hot there sometimes too. But even when it was very hot, she didn't wear her uniform open at the neck. That was against the rules. And it wasn't the way Marsha thought a Space Police commander should look.

Commander Kyle stood up. "Come on," he said to Marsha. "I'll show you around the station." Marsha followed him out of the office.

Outside it they met several police officers. They were checking the calls coming into the station. A woman in the group waved to Commander Kyle.

She called out to him, "Hello, Kyle!"

He waved to the woman. Then he looked at Marsha. When he saw the surprised look on her face, he asked, "What's the matter?"

"Nothing," she answered.

"Something's wrong," Commander Kyle said. "What is it?"

"It's just that I thought your officers would call you 'Commander,' " Marsha said. "Not just 'Kyle.' "

"Oh, so that's it," Commander Kyle said. "Well, we're all friends here. We don't worry

Graduation Day 19

about breaking a few rules that aren't really all that important."

Another officer asked, "Who's your friend, Kyle?"

"The new gun the Space Police School sent us," he said.

The woman who had spoken before asked, "Do you two want to join us in a game of ball?"

Commander Kyle asked Marsha, "How about it?"

Marsha said, "How can they play ball? Aren't those officers supposed to be checking the calls coming in to the station?"

"They *are* checking the calls," Commander Kyle said. "But that doesn't stop them from having a little fun at the same time."

"I'd rather get to work," Marsha said.

"Have it your way," Commander Kyle told her. Then he called an officer over to him. He asked the officer to show Marsha around the station. He told the man to show Marsha the job she would be doing on board the station. Then he went to play ball with the others.

NOISY ALIENS

Marsha was given the job of keeping track of every ship that flew near the station. She did her job well. And while she did it, she also learned all she could about the station. She used some of her free time to learn about the jobs the other officers had.

She didn't like everything she learned about the station and its officers. She also didn't like what she saw of Commander Kyle. She thought he should be less friendly with his officers. After all, he was their commander. But he often acted as if he were just another officer.

Marsha also thought that most of the officers on the station didn't seem to have their minds on their work. They seemed to be more interested in having fun than in doing their jobs. And Commander Kyle didn't seem to mind.

On the other hand, Marsha couldn't find anything wrong with the way the station worked. Calls to the station were always taken. Help was sent to ships in space that needed it. When a crime took place on one of the worlds near the station, an officer went there at once.

Still, Marsha couldn't help wishing that things on the station were more like they had been at the Space Police School. There everything was always kept clean. Uniforms were worn the way they were supposed to be worn. On the station, things were not always as clean as they should be. And many officers didn't wear their uniforms the way they were supposed to be worn.

But Marsha said nothing about these matters. It wasn't up to her to change them. If things were to change, Commander Kyle would have to change them.

Three days after coming to the station, Marsha sat tracking a ship that was flying past the station. She was so busy that at first she didn't see the red light flashing on her control board. But then she did see it. And she knew that the flashing red light could mean only one thing—trouble.

She found out what the trouble was when she heard Commander Kyle's voice come through the station's speakers.

"We've just had a call from the planet Sunworld," he said. "Aliens have landed there. They're causing trouble in the human settlement. I'm going to Sunworld at once to see what's needed. I want Officer Marsha Brody to come with me."

Marsha called to another officer. He came and took over for her on the control board. Then she ran to the station's dock. Commander Kyle was already on board a police cruiser. Marsha sat next to him as he flew the cruiser toward Sunworld.

When they reached the planet, Commander Kyle brought the cruiser down. Then he and Marsha got out.

"The human settlement is over there," he said. He pointed to it. "Let's go!"

As they ran toward the small human settlement they heard the sound of shots. Then they saw the bright flashes of light—flashes that could come only from laser guns. Marsha's hand went to her own laser gun. She followed Commander Kyle into the settlement.

The first thing they saw was a crowd of people. All of them were firing their laser guns. At first Marsha couldn't see what they were shooting at. She moved closer. Then she saw the aliens.

They were at the far end of the settlement. They were tall and completely covered with red feathers. But they had no wings. Each alien stood on two thin legs. Each had two arms with only two fingers on each hand. The fingers ended in sharp claws.

To Marsha, the aliens looked very ugly.

She looked around. Two aliens lay dead on the ground. Other aliens were trying to get to where the humans were. Marsha pointed her laser gun at the closest alien.

Commander Kyle ordered, "Hold your fire!"

Marsha said, "But those aliens are after the people!"

"Hold your fire," Commander Kyle said again.

Marsha watched as an alien grabbed a woman. The woman shot him. But another alien grabbed her from behind. The alien ran away with her. Other aliens grabbed other people. As they caught the humans, the aliens made loud noises. They seemed to yell at the humans. But Marsha couldn't understand what they were saying.

Commander Kyle yelled, "Let's move in!"

It's about time, Marsha thought to herself. The two ran toward the humans and the aliens that were trying to grab them.

The aliens saw Marsha and Commander Kyle coming toward them. They began to make even more noise. They waved their arms. They pointed at the sky.

Commander Kyle suddenly stopped. He turned on the small recorder that hung from his belt. He picked it up and pointed it toward the running aliens. In a few seconds he turned off his recorder.

Then all the aliens turned and ran. Marsha ran after them. Commander Kyle followed Marsha after the aliens.

Before they could catch them, the aliens boarded their spaceship. Its door closed. The alien ship left Sunworld and flew up into space.

"We could have brought a few of them down if we had fired our guns," Marsha said.

Commander Kyle said nothing. He just stood there and watched the ship until he could no longer see it.

"We could go after it," Marsha said.

Commander Kyle shook his head. "It's flying faster than our cruiser can fly. We'd never catch it. Let's go back and talk to the humans here. They'll be able to tell us what happened."

They walked back to the settlement. The people there were doing what they could to help those who had been hurt by the aliens. Many of the humans had been cut by the aliens' sharp claws.

A man was crying. Commander Kyle went up to him. He asked, "What happened here?"

The man's body shook. He covered his face with his hands. Commander Kyle asked him again to explain what had happened.

Finally the man took his hands away from his eyes. He said, "My wife—they got her. Those dirty aliens grabbed her and put her on their ship. I tried to save her. But I couldn't."

Commander Kyle asked the man, "Why did the aliens attack you?"

He shook his head. "They didn't have laser guns. They didn't shoot at us with anything. But they did hurt a lot of people when they tried to grab them. They hurt me." He showed Commander Kyle the cuts on his body. They had been made by the aliens' claws.

Commander Kyle asked the man, "What did the aliens do when they first landed?"

"They started making that loud noise you heard. None of us could understand what they were saying. Did you understand them?"

"No, I didn't," said Commander Kyle. He rubbed the side of his face. He looked up into the sky.

The man asked him, "Why don't you do something? Why are you just standing there like that? What good are you Space Police officers if you don't try to get back the people the aliens took?"

Marsha was thinking the same thing. She wanted to go after the alien ship. She didn't think that standing around asking a lot of questions would help bring the people back.

"We'll look into this matter," Commander Kyle told the man. "We'll try to get your wife and those other people back."

The man yelled, "When? Next year?"

Commander Kyle turned from the man. He spoke to Marsha. "You stay here. Find out everything you can about the attack. I'm going back to the station. I'll check things out from that end. Let me know what you find out here."

Marsha had to do as she was told. She watched Commander Kyle leave in the cruiser.

The man standing beside her spoke. "I hope I never need help from the Space Police again. What good are you? My wife's gone. So are a lot of other people. And that commander of yours—he just takes off without doing a thing."

Marsha said nothing. But she couldn't help thinking that the man was right.

BATTLE AT SUNWORLD

Marsha talked to a lot of the people who lived on Sunworld. She asked many questions about the planet. She learned many things.

She learned that Sunworld was one of five planets in orbit around its sun. The people had come to Sunworld long ago. There were no other kinds of life besides the humans who lived there.

But there were other kinds of life on the other four planets that circled the yellow sun. The people said that there were many strange animals on those planets.

Battle at Sunworld 29

Marsha asked the people if the aliens had come from one of the other planets. The people were sure that they hadn't. Many of them had visited the other four planets. There were no aliens there like the ones who had just attacked them.

Marsha called the people together. She told them that the aliens might attack them again. To keep themselves safe they must keep their laser guns ready. She told several people to stay outside the settlement and watch for signs of the alien spaceship.

Then she asked the people to take her to their communications center. When she got there she put in a call to Space Station Number Nine. She asked to speak to the station's computer.

She told the computer what had happened on Sunworld. She told it about the aliens—what they looked like, what their ship was like. She asked the computer to check its records for anything it knew about the aliens.

It took the computer some time to answer her. When it did, it said, "I have no record of such aliens. They do not live on any of the planets in this part of space."

Marsha said, "Are you sure? Their ship wasn't very big. It couldn't have come from another galaxy. So the aliens must have come from a planet near Sunworld. Check again, please."

She waited while the computer checked its records again. Then she heard it say, "I have no record of such aliens in any galaxy or on any planet that we know about."

Marsha left the communications center. As she walked through the settlement she passed a small space field. She kept wondering about the aliens. The computer knew nothing about them. So where could they have come from? And *why* had they come to Sunworld? Why had they taken away some of the people who lived on Sunworld?

Marsha looked up at the sky. She saw the big yellow sun. Suddenly she saw something more. At first she thought it was a big bird. Then it came closer. She saw that it wasn't a bird. It was the alien spaceship! It was coming back to Sunworld!

Just then a man ran up. He had been watching outside the settlement. He yelled at Marsha, "They're coming back!"

Battle at Sunworld 31

"I know," she said. "I see them. Help me get the people into their houses. Then you and the others who were watching for the aliens will help me fight them off."

The man ran to follow Marsha's orders. At the same time Marsha started running through the streets of the settlement. She told everyone she saw to stay inside their houses. She told them to get their laser guns ready. They might have to fight for their lives.

Soon the streets were empty. Quickly Marsha headed for the communications center. She wanted to tell Commander Kyle about the alien ship's return. But she didn't get far. As she ran she saw the alien ship set down on Sunworld. There was no time to make her call now.

She ran out of the settlement. She found the group of people who had been watching for the ship.

She told them, "Take cover! Stay down and out of sight!"

All the people dropped to the ground. They found places to hide behind big rocks. Marsha felt very hot as she dropped down behind a rock. She guessed she was hot because she had been running around the settlement so much.

"Wait until the aliens get close to us," she told the people with her. "We don't want to waste any of our fire power."

Everyone watched the alien ship. A door opened in its side. An alien came out and looked around. Then a few more aliens came to the door. Marsha could hear them talking to one another. But she couldn't understand what they said.

Then the aliens began to walk toward the settlement.

"They still don't have any guns," Marsha whispered to the people. "Let me talk to them. Maybe we can catch them. Let's try. Then we can find out what they've done with the people they took. We can go on board their ship."

The aliens came closer. Soon they were almost to the place where the people were hiding. Marsha stood up. She pointed her laser gun at the aliens.

She said, "Stop!"

When the aliens saw her laser gun, they stopped. Then they began to make their noise. They waved their arms toward the sky.

Marsha looked up at the sky. There was nothing there but the sun.

Then the aliens pointed to their ship. Marsha didn't know what they were trying to show her. She tried hard to understand them. But she couldn't.

She yelled at the aliens, "Can you understand *me?*"

The aliens waved their arms toward the sky again. Again they pointed to their ship. And then they pointed at Marsha.

Marsha yelled to the people hiding near her. "Let's try to get them!" The people jumped up. All of them held laser guns in their hands.

The aliens didn't move at first. But then they began to walk slowly toward the people. When they got close they rushed forward.

Marsha yelled at them, *"Stop!"* But she could tell that they weren't going to stop.

Then a man yelled at the top of his voice. "Kill them all! Don't let them get any of you! Kill these aliens and then we'll rush their ship!"

Marsha turned to see who had yelled. It was the man whose wife had been taken away by the aliens when they came the first time.

Some of the people began to shoot. The aliens ducked the laser fire and kept on coming. Then one of the aliens was hit. But each of the others grabbed a person. They ran with them toward their ship.

The people who had not been caught kept firing at the aliens.

Marsha yelled, "Stop firing! You might hit one of your own people!"

Her words made the people stop shooting. They watched as the aliens boarded their ship with the people they had caught.

Marsha was mad. She decided that she wouldn't just stand by and let the aliens fly away with those people. She was going to stop them. But then she had an idea.

She turned and ran back into the settlement. She raced to the space field. When she got there she boarded a small ship. She took her place at the controls. Quickly she fired the ship's jets. The ship shot up into the sky.

Then Marsha flew the ship down toward Sunworld. She could see the alien ship below her. She circled in the sky and waited. Soon the alien ship lifted off. In a minute it was far above Sunworld. Marsha followed it.

A WATER CITY

As Marsha followed the alien ship, she felt good. She was doing something to help the people. She wasn't just standing around asking a lot of questions. What she planned to do might not work. She knew that. But Commander Kyle had done nothing. She would do something.

A smile crossed her face. If her plan did work, she would enjoy telling Commander Kyle about it. She was sure he'd be surprised to hear her story. He probably thought she would stay on Sunworld. He probably thought she was still there asking the people questions. Well, he'll find out how wrong he was, she thought. It might teach him a lesson. Commander Kyle just might learn something about how police officers *should* do their work.

Marsha kept on following the alien ship. She wondered where it was headed. She could see no planets through the windows of her ship. Only a few stars.

Suddenly she found herself getting very close to the alien ship. She looked down at her control board. The speed of her ship was the same as it had been. The alien ship must be slowing down, she thought. So she slowed her ship, too.

Then it happened.

There was a bright flash of white light all around the alien ship. Marsha thought the ship had exploded. But it hadn't. It flew right through the white light. Then it was gone from sight.

Marsha didn't know what had happened to it. But she was afraid of that flash of white light. She tried to slow her ship. She tried to turn to the side. Before she could do either, she

A Water City 37

found herself in a flash of bright white light. It was all around her ship. She covered her eyes because the strong light hurt them.

In a few seconds she took her hands away from her eyes. The white light was gone. So were the stars that she had seen through her ship's window a few minutes ago. Now Marsha found herself flying over the most beautiful city she had ever seen. She looked down at it. She knew for sure that the city had not been made by humans.

It was very different from any human city she had ever seen. Its buildings were blue and white. On top of each one was a gold ball. Instead of streets, blue water ran through the city. Marsha saw some aliens swimming in the water.

Just then something caught her eye. The alien ship was setting down outside the city.

Marsha flew over the ship. Then she set her ship down behind a hill. She hoped the aliens hadn't seen her. She left her ship and ran toward theirs.

As she ran, the aliens left their ship. They went into their city. Some jumped into the blue water and began to swim.

When Marsha reached the alien ship, she saw that the door was open. She looked inside. None of the people the aliens had caught on Sunworld were there. Marsha wondered if the flash of white light had killed them. But it hadn't killed her. Where were they? For that matter, where was she? What world was this?

She decided she had no time to worry about the answers to her questions. She made her way into the aliens' ship. She moved slowly. In her hand was her laser gun. She walked down an empty hall. Then she turned a corner. She came face to face with one of the aliens!

Before the alien could do anything, Marsha used her gun. She didn't shoot it. She used it to hit the alien on the side of the head. The alien fell to the floor and didn't move.

Good, Marsha thought. I don't want to have to shoot. If I do, the sound of my shots will bring other aliens.

She ran through the ship looking for the people the aliens had caught. She looked in one room after another. At last she came to the bottom of the ship. There she found the people. She also found other kinds of life. There were strange animals. There were things that looked like plants. But they made noises when they saw Marsha.

Marsha yelled to the people, "Come on! I've come to take you out of here."

A woman said, "But we can't get out! The aliens have set up a force field to keep us in here."

Marsha looked around. Where was the force field's control button? She found it on a wall near her. She pressed the button. Then she walked toward the people. The force field was gone.

"It's OK now," she told the people. "Let's move fast. Follow me!"

The people followed Marsha to the top of the ship. In front of them was the door that led out of the ship. But between the people and the door was the alien Marsha had hit. And the alien was waking up!

Marsha ran forward. She hit the alien again with her laser gun. He fell. She told the people, "The alien's out cold! Let's get out of here!"

She ran out of the ship. All the people followed her. All of them ran toward Marsha's ship. But near the ship they saw a group of aliens. The aliens had found Marsha's ship. They were standing around looking at it.

When Marsha saw the aliens, she told the people what to do. Then she fired into the air. The sound of her shot caused the aliens to turn. They saw Marsha. They began to move toward her. She fired at the ground in front of them. The aliens moved back.

While she fired, the people ran for Marsha's ship. When all of them were on board, Marsha ran toward the ship, too. As she ran past the aliens, they tried to grab her. One of them caught her. But she hit the alien's hand with her gun and broke away.

Finally she got to her ship. She fired again at the ground in front of the aliens as the doors closed. Again they jumped back out of the line of fire.

Marsha went to her ship's control board. She pressed several buttons. The ship's jets fired. Soon the ship was high in the sky.

But Marsha had a problem and she knew it. She didn't know how to find her way back to Sunworld. She had never been where she was now. She had no star map to show her the way home. To make matters even worse, she saw the alien ship flying after her.

She flew as fast as she could. She hoped she was going toward Sunworld. The alien ship stayed close behind her.

All at once there was a bright flash of white light. It was all around Marsha's ship. Then it was gone. And suddenly Marsha found her ship flying through a part of space she had seen before.

She had made it! She felt like yelling for joy. But she didn't when she saw a flash of white light coming from behind her. She turned. The alien ship was flying through the white light. It was coming after Marsha's ship.

VOICES FROM THE FUTURE

Marsha flew her ship at its top speed. That was fast enough to keep the alien ship from catching up. As she flew she kept her eyes on her ship's control board. It told her Sunworld wasn't too far away. Soon she saw the planet coming up fast.

She got ready to land. As she brought her ship down she told the people to make a run for the settlement. She also told them to tell the people in the settlement that the aliens were coming. As soon as she landed, the people ran out. Marsha got her ship's guns ready. She planned to try to stop the alien ship from landing on Sunworld. Marsha fired at it.

The alien ship came close. It tried to make a landing. She kept it from landing.

Suddenly she saw another ship in the sky. It was a big one. She knew what it was. It was one of the police cruisers from Space Station Number Nine. She thought the alien ship might try to attack it.

I must stop that ship from attacking, Marsha thought. She fired her guns again. Her shots hit the ship. It rolled in space, first one way and then the other. It seemed to be trying to turn around. But it couldn't. It was rolling too fast.

Just then the police cruiser set down on Sunworld next to Marsha's ship. Marsha was glad to see it. Now more fire power was at hand. The guns of the two ships should be able to destroy the alien ship.

Marsha saw Commander Kyle jump out of the cruiser. He was by himself. He waved to Marsha to come down from her ship. She got out and went to meet him. As she walked she was surprised to find that it was very hot outside her ship.

When she reached Commander Kyle she told him that the aliens were trying to attack Sunworld again.

"But I hit their ship several times," she said. "It's in pretty bad shape. It looks like it's going to crash-land."

Commander Kyle looked mad. He started to say something. But before he could speak the alien ship crash-landed on Sunworld. It began to burn. Aliens ran from it. One of them was on fire. The others tried to save the burning alien. But it was too late. The alien burned up completely.

Marsha took out her laser gun. "They'll probably try to take us now," she said to Commander Kyle.

Just then the people ran out of the settlement. All of them had laser guns. They began to fire at the aliens. The aliens turned and ran. Some of them found cover from the people's fire. But some didn't. Those who didn't were killed.

Commander Kyle yelled at the people. He told them to stop shooting. But they didn't. Then Marsha got ready to fire at the aliens. But before she could get off even one shot,

Voices from the Future 45

Commander Kyle knocked her gun from her hand.

She yelled at him, "What did you do that for?"

"Listen to me," he said. "Listen very carefully. Those aliens aren't trying to hurt the people of Sunworld. They're trying to *save* them!"

Marsha said, "Save them? But they took some of the people away to their own world. I had to go to their world to bring those people back."

"You should have left them there," Commander Kyle said.

"Why? I don't understand you!"

"Because those aliens are from the future. Their world is hundreds of years in the future. They know something that the people here don't."

Marsha was so surprised she couldn't speak.

Commander Kyle went on. "I tried to call you through Sunworld's communications center. But you didn't answer. So I came here. I wanted to tell you and the people about the aliens. One of my officers understands the way the aliens speak. I played her a recording of their talk that I made when I was here before. The officer told me what the aliens were saying."

Marsha asked, "What were they saying?"

"They were telling the people here that they must leave Sunworld. The other kinds of life on the other four planets in orbit around this sun have already left their homes. The aliens have saved them."

Marsha asked, "Saved them from what?"

She couldn't hear Commander Kyle's answer—loud noises blocked it out.

He ordered Marsha, "Come with me! We've got to stop those people from killing any more aliens!" He began to run toward the crowd of people. Marsha ran right beside him.

When they got close to the people, Commander Kyle fired his gun at the ground in front of them. The people stopped shooting at the aliens. They looked at Commander Kyle.

Then a man in the crowd of people yelled to Commander Kyle. He asked the commander, "Why are you stopping us? Why don't you help us? Together we can wipe out these aliens once and for all!"

Commander Kyle asked him, "Do you feel how hot it is here now?"

"What does that have to do with the aliens? Sure, it's hot," the man said. "The sun's out."

"That's not the reason it's so hot," Commander Kyle said. "It's hot because—"

The man turned away. He started firing at the aliens again.

Commander Kyle stepped toward him. He grabbed the man's arm. "If you fire once more, I'll shoot you," he said.

The man just looked at Commander Kyle. He asked, "Whose side are you on? What is it with you and those aliens? Why are you sticking up for them?"

"I'll tell you," Commander Kyle said. "But first you must stop shooting." Then he spoke to the man and the other people in the crowd.

"All of you must leave Sunworld. And I mean right now. As fast as you can. Get on board the police cruiser. There's room enough for all of you."

A woman said, "Leave? Why should we leave? This is our home."

"Get on board the cruiser," Commander Kyle said. "If you don't, you'll all die."

The man who had spoken before asked, "You mean the aliens will kill us? We won't let them. Why, they don't even have any guns. We'll wipe these crazy aliens out in a few more minutes."

"*You'll* be wiped out in a few more minutes if you don't get on board the cruiser," Commander Kyle said. "You sun is about to explode! Now *move!*"

Then Commander Kyle said, "Marsha, get the aliens on board the cruiser. Quick!"

Marsha had never seen Commander Kyle like this before. His eyes burned. When he moved he moved fast. When he spoke his words came fast. He seemed to know what to do. Marsha couldn't believe that he was the same person she had met on the space station several days ago.

She ran toward the aliens to lead them to the cruiser. As she did, some of the people who hadn't heard Commander Kyle's words fired at them.

Marsha heard Commander Kyle yell at the people who had fired. "If you hit that officer or any of those aliens, you'll be shot next!" The shooting stopped.

Finally Marsha reached the aliens. They were still hiding behind some rocks. She pointed at them and then she pointed to the cruiser. At first the aliens didn't seem to understand her. So she pointed at them again and then again to the cruiser. She walked toward the cruiser. She waved to the aliens to come with her.

They stood up slowly. Then they followed her to the cruiser. As they did they kept looking back at the people with the laser guns.

When the aliens were all on board the cruiser, Marsha heard a woman talking to Commander Kyle. She said, "I just don't believe you!"

"It's true," he said to the woman. "What I've just told you is true. If you people don't get on board that cruiser you'll all die. Your sun is going to explode any minute!"

THE SUN GOES WILD

The woman asked Commander Kyle, "How do you know that?"

"The aliens said so," he answered.

"But how do *they* know? They're only aliens, after all."

"Those aliens have come to our time from the future," Commander Kyle explained. "Their history books tell what happened to Sunworld and the other four planets in orbit around its sun. The history books say that the sun exploded on this very day. The aliens came here through a Time Gate to tell you—and to save you."

Someone in the crowd asked, "What's a Time Gate?"

"The aliens said it's like a door in time," Commander Kyle answered. "It lets them move in time as well as in space."

Marsha said, "That flash of white light! That must have happened when we passed through the Time Gate." She told Commander Kyle about the bright light she had gone through twice.

"The light is pretty bright here," said someone in the crowd. "And it sure is getting hot."

Everyone looked up. The sun in the sky was very bright. It wasn't yellow now. It had turned red.

"The sun looks so strange," said a man in the crowd. "It's never looked like that before."

"We have no time to waste," Commander Kyle said to the people. "I can't force you to leave with me. But I hope all of you will come. Because if you don't, you'll die."

"I believe him," someone in the crowd said. "Look at the sun. And besides those aliens didn't try to hurt us. I know they took some of our people away. But I think now that they were trying to save them."

"Let's get on board the cruiser," said a woman. She went to it and boarded. Several other people followed.

"I'll be right back," said a man near Commander Kyle. He turned and started running toward the settlement.

Commander Kyle asked him, "Where are you going? Come back here!"

The man yelled as he ran away, "My sister's in the settlement! I've got to get her!"

Commander Kyle yelled after him, "There isn't time! Look at the sun! It's going to explode any minute now!"

But the man didn't stop. He kept running toward the settlement.

As he left, most of the people in the crowd ran toward the cruiser. But some of them stayed where they were. Commander Kyle and Marsha tried to talk them into getting on board the cruiser. But they wouldn't listen. They said they just didn't believe that their sun was going to explode. They thought the aliens' story about the sun was a lie. Or a trick.

The Sun Goes Wild 53

"Very well," Commander Kyle said. "Come on, Marsha." They ran to the cruiser.

Once inside, Commander Kyle fired the ship's jets. Marsha looked out the window. Suddenly she jumped up.

She said to Commander Kyle, "There's the man who went to get his sister! He and a woman are running for the cruiser!"

Just then all the aliens on the cruiser began to make their noise. They pointed through the windows at the sun.

Commander Kyle looked at the sun. Then he said, "We've got to go right now. We've got to get away from that sun before it kills us!"

He took the ship up.

Marsha looked back at the people left behind on Sunworld. She wished they were on board the ship with her. Her heart went out to them. But soon she could no longer see them. The cruiser was far from Sunworld.

Now Sunworld looked like a small ball in space. Near it was another ball—a big red one. The red ball was the sun. Sunworld and four other planets circled around it.

As Marsha watched, the sun suddenly seemed to grow very big. Then it exploded. Big pieces of the sun flew through space. The pieces burned brightly. They hit Sunworld and the four other planets. All of the planets exploded.

Marsha turned away from the sight. In her mind she could see the man who had tried to save his sister. She closed her eyes. She thought about the people she had brought back from the aliens' world. She wondered if they had all stayed on Sunworld and died.

"It's over," Commander Kyle said. "We did all we could." He looked at Marsha and saw that her eyes were closed.

"You did what you thought was right," he said to her in a soft voice. "You tried to save the people you thought the aliens would hurt."

Marsha opened her eyes. She looked at Commander Kyle. "But what I did was wrong," she said. "I —"

"You didn't understand the aliens," said Commander Kyle.

"You didn't either—at first," Marsha said. "But you tried to find out what they were saying before you did anything. And you did find out. If you hadn't, *everyone* who had been on Sunworld would be dead now. I'd probably be dead, too."

Commander Kyle's eyes met Marsha's. He didn't say anything. But Marsha did. She felt she had to say what was on her mind. She felt she had to clear the air between her and Commander Kyle.

"When I first came to Space Station Number Nine, I thought you didn't know how to run it," she said. "You didn't wear your uniform the way you're supposed to. You didn't seem to act the way I thought a commander in the Space Police should."

"Well, I do like to play ball with my officers now and then," Commander Kyle said. He almost smiled.

Marsha went on. "You didn't follow all the rules. But you were the one who saved us all."

"I just waited to act until I had all the facts," Commander Kyle said. "I don't like to act on something before I know all there is to know. I like to be careful."

I like to be careful.

The words of her teacher at the Space Police School rang in Marsha's mind:

"To be a good Space Police officer you've got to be smart. But that's not enough. You've also got to be careful."

Marsha looked at Commander Kyle. He is smart, she thought. So am I. But Commander Kyle is careful, too. He found out all the facts about the aliens before he moved. But I acted without all the facts.

She looked at the aliens. She thought about how hard they had tried to save the people of Sunworld. They had tried and it had cost some of them their lives. She was surprised to find that the aliens no longer looked ugly to her.

She looked back at Commander Kyle. She no longer minded the fact that he wore his uniform the wrong way. She didn't think she would mind it if he didn't always follow all the rules.

Commander Kyle spoke to her. "This is your first job as a Space Police officer. You've learned from it, I'm sure."

"I have," Marsha said. "And I've also learned a lot from you."

"Maybe you'd like to learn more—like how to play a real good game of ball. I could teach you after we take these aliens back to their world and after we take care of the Sunworld people who came with us."

"I'd like that," Marsha said.

"You're on then," Commander Kyle told her. "Now let's see if I can find the Time Gate that leads to the future."

"I can take you to it," Marsha said. "I remember the way."

"Good," Commander Kyle said. "And since you know the way, why don't you take over the controls of the cruiser?"

Marsha headed toward the future.